Dear Teachers, Carers, Parents, and GrandParents too!

Over half the world's children are bilingual. Young children pick up their own and a foreign language effortlessly if we give them the right type of opportunities.

This interactive story about naughty Léo, who only speaks French, will help children learn simple, but useful, French quickly.

In the story children hear:
* narration which includes some words and simple phrases in French.
* Léo's simple replies.

Léo's speech is on lift-up flaps with the English translation underneath. By lifting up the flap the child becomes physically involved in the story, which makes absorbing Léo's language easier.

A game provides an added opportunity to use the story language in a fun way. The glossary helps with the pronunciation of the simple French vocabulary.

As in the initial stages of learning their home language, children need time to absorb French before they are ready to say it. Read the story in the same way as you read any picture storybook in your home language encouraging children to join in. When they are ready they may surprise you by saying Léo's reply and gradually taking over his role.

When you are reading the narration use a quieter voice for the English to indicate that it is not a vital part of the story. Once children know the narration, the English translation can be left out as they no longer need it!

Success motivates: it also makes children happy. Be generous with praise, as what you share successfully today will create positive long-term attitudes to learning and using a foreign language.

Enjoy Léo together – he's fun!

Opal Dunn

Look! There's Léo. He's coming to school.
Léo only speaks French, so we'll talk to him in French.
Listen.

Salut. *Hi*

Salut Léo. *Hi Léo*

Léo's got a big bag. Let's tell him to put it on the table.

Mets-le sur la table. *Put it on the table.*
Sur la table. *On the table.*

Now let's ask him to sit down.

Assieds-toi. *Sit down.*

Assieds-toi, Léo. *Sit down, Léo.*

Oh dear! Look at Léo. No, Léo.

Non, Léo. *No, Léo.*

Pas sur la table. *Not on the table.*

Sur la chaise. *On the chair.*

**D'accord
Sur la chaise**

Look! Léo's opening his bag. What's inside?

Une balle. *A ball.*
Une balle rouge. *A red ball.*

Rouge

And look! Another ball.

Une balle jaune. *A yellow ball.*

And another ball? What colour is it?

Bleu. *Blue.*

Oh dear! Léo's lost the red ball.

Où est la balle rouge? *Where is the red ball?*

La balle rouge. *The red ball.*

Look! It's there.

Sous la chaise. *Under the chair.*

Sous la chaise, Léo. *Under the chair, Léo.*

Look! Léo's putting the three balls in the bag.

Dans le sac. *In the bag.*

Now let's ask Léo to play a game with us.

Tu veux jouer? *Do you want to play?*

Oui

Let's look at the cards.

Arrête, Léo. *Stop, Léo.*

Tu veux jouer encore? *Do you want to play again?*

Non merci

Au revoir

Combien? – How many?

This is a type of memory game. Players have to pick up a pair of matching cards. The winner is the player with the most pairs of cards. Use the cards in the story as models to make your own cards.

Place the cards face down on the table. The first player picks up a card and as she shows it she says the number in French. She then places it face upwards on the table. She picks up a second card and says the number. If both the numbers are the same, she keeps the pair. If the numbers are different she puts them back on the table face downwards.

The next player does the same. The game continues until there are no cards left on the table. The players then count their pairs of cards to find the winner. Begin with numbers 1 to 3 and gradually add numbers up to 10.

The game can also be played with colour cards or pictures on cards.

There are many types of spoken French as there are spoken English, and this pronunciation guide is only an approximation to help you speak French with your child.
The list includes the French words for objects you see in the illustrations.
This will give you the answer to the child's question when looking at the pictures –
What's that in French? **Qu'est-ce que c'est en français?**

French	Pronunciation	English	French	Pronunciation	English
Arrête	*a-ret*	Stop	**Ici**	*ee-see*	Here
Assieds-toi	*ass-yay-twa*	Sit down	**Jaune**	*joh-ne*	Yellow
Au revoir	*or rev-waar*	Goodbye	**Je ne sais pas**	*jer ner say pa*	I don't know
Balle (la)	*bal*	Ball	**Le / La**	*ler / lah*	The
Bleu	*bler*	Blue	**Léo**	*lay-oh*	Léo
Bonjour	*bon-joor*	Hello	**Livre (le)**	*leev-ruh*	Book
Carte (la)	*kart*	Cards	**Lunettes (les)**	*loo-net*	Glasses
Casquette (la)	*cas-ket*	Cap	**Mets-le**	*meh-ler*	Put it
Chaise (la)	*shez*	Chair	**Merci**	*mer-see*	Thank you
Chat (le)	*sha*	Cat	**Non**	*non*	No
Crayon (le)	*kra-yon*	Pencil	**Oiseau (l')**	*wa-zoh*	Bird
Crocodile (le)	*kro-co-dil*	Crocodile	**Où est**	*oo eh*	Where is
D'accord	*da-kor*	OK	**Oui**	*wee*	Yes
Dans	*don*	In	**Ours (l')**	*oors*	Bear
Ecole (l')	*eh-col*	School	**Papier (le)**	*pap-i-yeh*	Paper
Encore	*on-kor*	Again	**Pas**	*pa*	Not
Et	*eh*	And	**Porte (la)**	*port*	Door

French	Pronunciation	English	French	Pronunciation	English
Pour	*poor*	For	Un	*uhn*	1
Rouge	*roo-je*	Red	Deux	*duh*	2
Sac (le)	*sack*	Bag	Trois	*twa*	3
Salut	*sa-loo*	Hi	Quatre	*katr*	4
Souris (la)	*soo-ree*	Mouse	Cinq	*sank*	5
Sous	*soo*	Under	Six	*seess*	6
Sur	*soor*	On	Sept	*set*	7
Table (la)	*ta-bluh*	Table	Huit	*wheet*	8
Tigre (le)	*ti-gruh*	Tiger	Neuf	*nerf*	9
Toi	*twa*	You	Dix	*deess*	10
T-shirt	*tee-shurt*	T-shirt	Vingt	*van*	20
Tu veux jouer?	*too ver joo-ay?*	Do you want to play?	Trente	*tront*	30
			Quarante	*ka-ront*	40
Un / Une	*uhn / oon*	A	Cinquante	*san-kont*	50
Vite	*veet*	Hurry up	Cent	*s-on*	100
Voici	*vwa-see*	Here you are			

For Sabrina and Richard Dunn – O.D.

Léo le Chat goes to school! copyright © Frances Lincoln Limited 2006
Concept and text copyright © Opal Dunn 2006
Illustrations copyright © Cathy Gale 2006

First published in Great Britain in 2006 and in the USA in 2007
by Frances Lincoln Children's Books, 4 Torriano Mews,
Torriano Avenue, London NW5 2RZ

www.franceslincoln.com

Distributed in the USA by Publishers Group West

All rights reserved.
British Library Cataloguing in Publication Data available on request

ISBN 10: 1-84507-403-3
ISBN 13: 978-1-84507-403-6

Printed in China

1 3 5 7 9 8 6 4 2